RUSSIAN FOLK TALE

A series
of Fairy Tales
SMALL BOOKS
WITH BIG PICTURES
for Toddlers
who are learning
to read.

Fairy Tale
Gingerbread House.

Author: I. Kraus
Illustator: A. Kraus

ISBN: 979-8-5841-0761-1

Author Page: amazon.com/author/kraus
email: krausigor3@gmail.com

RUSSIAN FOLK TALE

GINGERBREAD HOUSE

Retold by I. Kraus
Illustrated by A. Kraus

Once upon a time
in a tiny village,
there lived a brother
and sister named
Ivan and Masha.

One day they decided
to pick some berries,
so they grabbed their
baskets and went into
the forest.

They walked long
the path and suddenly
saw a clearing,
and in the center,
they saw a little
gingerbread house.
Its walls were made
of gingerbread, its roof
of lollipops. There was
no one around.

The children ran
straight to the little house
and started eating its
walls and then climbed
on the roof for lollipops.
Suddenly, someone
growled from inside
the house.

The owner of this
gingerbread house was
a bear. He heard the children
and yelled,
«Who is breaking my beloved
gingerbread house?»
The children got frightened
and ran, and the bear
ran after them. He chased
them, growling,
«I'll catch you!»

HONEY

The children dropped
their baskets of berries
and ran up a hill.
The angry bear was
close, and about
to catch them at any
moment.

The children ran to
a bush of nuts and asked,
«Can you hide us?
A big bear wants to catch us!»
«Get under my branches,
I'll hide you!» said the bush.
The children sat under
the bush, and the bear
ran past.

After the sound of
the bear's footsteps ceased,
the children crawled out,
and picked some nuts before
thanking the bush;
then they continued walking.
But the bear turned around
and saw the children,
and started chasing
them again.

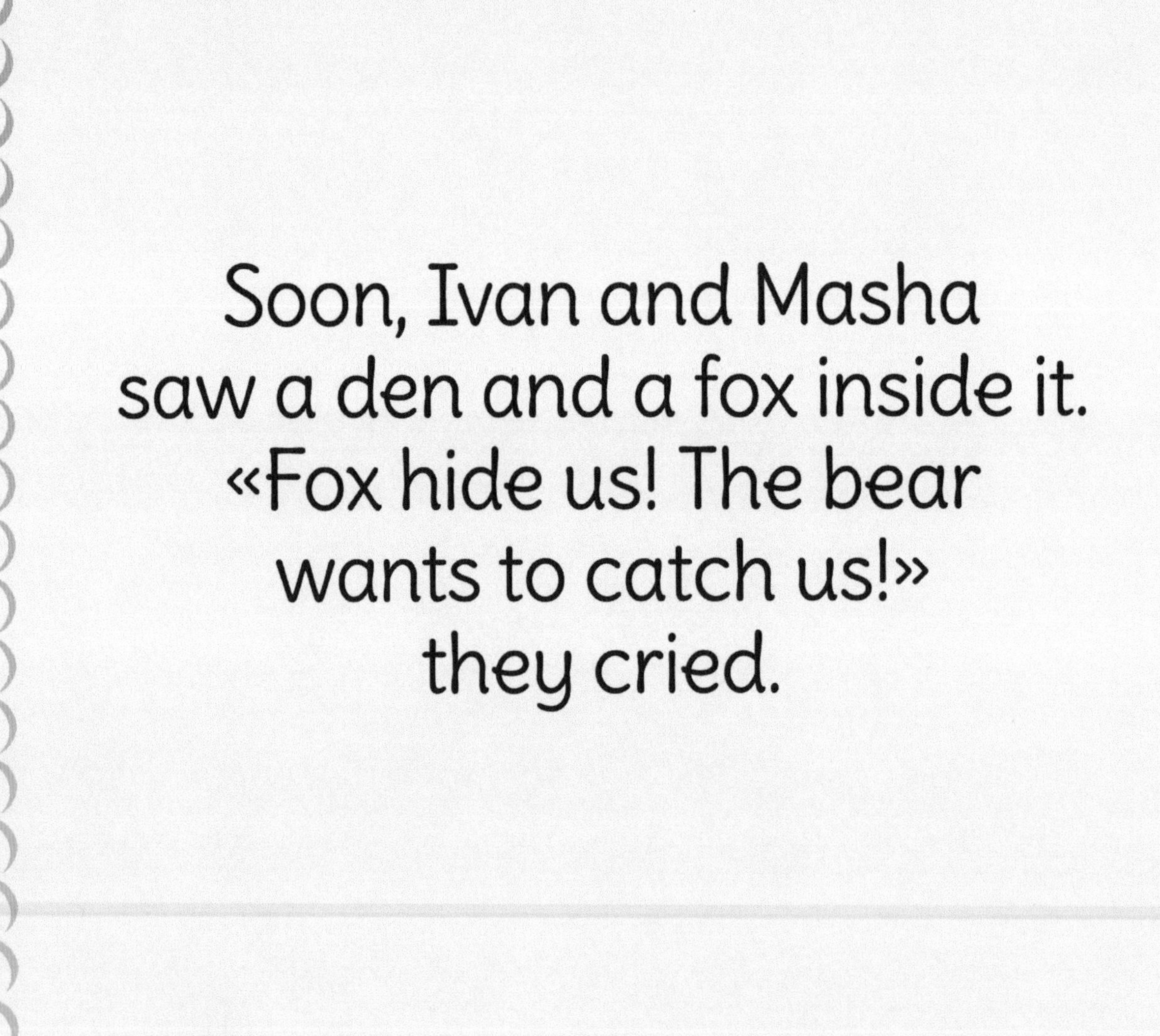

Soon, Ivan and Masha
saw a den and a fox inside it.
«Fox hide us! The bear
wants to catch us!»
they cried.

The fox hid the children,
and the bear ran past.
The children looked around
before they thanked the fox,
gave her some nuts,
and started home.

Meanwhile, the bear
was hiding in the bushes
waiting for children to come
out from their shelter.
He jumped out of the bushes
and chased them again.
«You won't escape children!»
he growled.

The children ran
to the river and saw there
was nowhere to go.
What do they do?
The bear was close. Suddenly,
they saw two ducks
in the water.
«Help us, ducks, take us to
the other side! A big bear
is about to catch us!»

The ducks put
the children on their
backs and took them
to the other side.

When the bear
reached the river, he saw
children on the other
bank. He waved his
paws and growled
with anger, but in vain.
The children escaped.

SEE YOU SOON IN THE NEXT FAIRY TALE
The End
BOOKS FOR KIDS

Printed in Great Britain
by Amazon